E
MAR

a minedition book
published by Penguin Young Readers Group

Text copyright © 2004 by Jane Goodall
Illustrations copyright © 2004 by Alan Marks
Coproduction with Michael Neugebauer Publishing Ltd. Hong Kong.

Published simultaneously in Canada.
Manufactured in Hong Kong by Wide World Ltd.
Designed by Michael Neugebauer
Typesetting in Nueva, designed by Carol Twombly
Color separation by Fotoreproduzioni Grafiche, Verona, Italy.

Library of Congress Cataloging-in-Publication Data available upon request.

ISBN 0-698-40002-X
10 9 8 7 6 5 4 3 2 1
First Impression

For more information please visit our website: www.minedition.com

and

Jane Goodall

Rickie

Henri

Pictures by
Alan Marks

A True Story

*R*ickie was born in the rain forest of Central Africa.

For the first two years she lived with her mother and the other chimpanzees of the community. Her mother was the center of Rickie's world. She carried her from place to place; she comforted her when she was hurting or frightened. Every hour or so— more often if she wanted—Rickie could drink the good warm milk from her mother's breasts.

Perhaps she had an older brother or sister; perhaps her grandmother was alive. We shall never know.

Because one day—probably at first light, when the chimpanzees were starting to leave their night nests and feed—a loud bang disturbed the peace of the forest. Rickie's mother fell to the ground, dead or mortally wounded.

Screaming in terror, Rickie clung tightly to her mother, who had never before let her down. But she could not help Rickie now. She would never help her again. The hunter seized Rickie and pushed her into a tiny basket, while the infant chimpanzee, who didn't understand, went on screaming and screaming for her mother.

The long journey through the forest, cramped in a little basket, must have been a nightmare for Rickie. She was hungry, but there was no warm, comforting milk. She was frightened. And she was hurting because shotgun pellets were lodged in her little body. But however much she cried, there was no one to help.

Eventually Rickie was tipped roughly out of the basket. She stared around in bewilderment. Everywhere there were huge people crowding close and staring at her, laughing in loud voices. Rickie was being offered for sale in one of the markets of Brazzaville, in the Congo Republic. It was hot, and she was tired and thirsty. Her wounds were hurting even more. Desperately she looked around for her mother, crying softly. But her mother did not come, and none of the people understood.

Rickie stopped crying and curled up on the ground. She closed her eyes. The tall, distinguished Congolese man who stopped presently to look at her thought that maybe the little chimpanzee infant was dead. He bent down and touched her. She opened her eyes. She was too tired and weak to be frightened.

The tall man knew that it was against the law to capture and sell infant chimpanzees. He was angry and threatened the hunter, saying that he would report him to the officials. The hunter, who probably didn't even know the law of the land, was scared and ran off, leaving Rickie behind.

So the tall man picked up Rickie, who was stiff with terror.
He wrapped his jacket around her and carried her back
to his house. As he went up the steps, his shaggy dog,
Henri, sniffed at the strange smelling creature in his
master's jacket. He growled a little, then curled up and
went back to sleep.

The tall man was very kind to Rickie. He found out the right food for an infant chimpanzee, and fed her good meals. He asked a doctor to take the shotgun pellets from her neck and back. And gradually some of her joy in life returned. Of course, she must have often thought about her mother and her life in the forest, but she learned to make the best of her new way of living—part of a human family.

The tall man was her guardian, and Rickie loved him best. She was terribly upset when he had to go away on a business trip. The rest of his family did not like her in the house. They went on feeding her, but they shut her outside. Good food is certainly necessary for an infant chimpanzee, but just like a human child, Rickie needed affectionate contact with a caring adult.
She needed love.

In her desperation she turned to the only adult she could find—
Henri, the dog. She went over to him as he sat watching her, and
reached out to hold his fur. At first he was scared—each time
she reached out, he growled a little and moved away. But
eventually he let her hold on to him.

And when he lay to sleep, she lay beside him, still holding on to
his fur.

What a lovely picture they made: a small black chimpanzee with huge sad eyes clinging tightly to a medium-sized brown shaggy dog whose bright eyes peered onto the world through his thick fringe of curly fur.

When Henri went around the streets of Brazzaville, scrounging food from the dustbins—as all real dogs will do if they have an opportunity—Rickie went with him.

She rode on his back, clinging on tight with arms and legs. Just as if she was riding on her mother.

And at night she snuggled close beside
him, holding his fur even when she was asleep.

For several weeks Rickie and Henri could be seen together in the
streets, or in the back garden of the big house where they lived.
And then the tall man came back. Rickie was very pleased to
see him, and hugged and kissed him for a long time. But she still
spent lots of time riding about on Henri, and sleeping close
beside him when her human guardian was at work.

At last the time came when Rickie was too big and heavy for Henri. It was very important for her to live with others of her kind so that she could learn chimpanzee behavior, chimpanzee manners. And so, though sad to part with her, her guardian sent her to a sanctuary where many orphans like herself were cared for. Soon Rickie made many new friends.

And what about Henri? Wasn't he sad, losing his chimpanzee friend? He was, of course. But not for long.

The tall man felt sorry for his little brown dog, and so he found a new friend—another dog, dark and about the same size as Henri.

So everyone was happy at the end…

Postscript

It was in 1993 that Rickie arrived at the Jane Goodall Institute's Tchimpounga Sanctuary, near Point Noire in the Congo Republic. It is our biggest sanctuary — there were 115 orphans when I visited in July 2003. Rickie is a healthy adolescent today.

The country around the sanctuary is beautiful, a mixture of forest and savanna stretching down to the unspoiled shore of the Atlantic Ocean. Quite a few wild chimpanzees are still living there, and we are working with the government to protect the whole area.

If only we could set our orphans free there. But sadly, this is not possible. There are too many villages. Our chimpanzees would approach people and might either be hurt, or hurt someone. Moreover, wild chimpanzees protect their territory fiercely from strangers and would probably kill our orphans. We are trying to find a forest far from people and wild chimpanzees, but this is not easy. There are not many places like that, certainly not ones suitable for chimpanzees to live.

If you would like to learn more about Tchimpounga and our other sanctuaries (in Uganda, Kenya, and South Africa), and about the work of the Jane Goodall Institute, check our website at www.janegoodall.org.

You can also learn how you could help us to care for Rickie. Once she needed Henri — now she needs you. So do all the other orphans like her.

Lots of love,

Jane Goodall